Piglet Shows
Some Talent

Adapted from a story by Hallie Marshall

Illustrations by John Kurtz

One day, Pooh and Piglet were visiting Owl. As Owl talked and talked and talked, Pooh began to doze off.

"Let's have a talent show!" Owl said. "Everyone can do something. I will, of course, offer my services as director."

"But what will I do?" Piglet asked.

"Now, now," Owl told him, "I'll teach you the dance of the fifty feathers—a show my great-uncle would perform to cheering crowds. You'll catch on in no time."

The next day, Owl tried to teach Piglet the dance of the fifty feathers. But Piglet could barely manage with two.

"It's just as well," Pooh told his friend. "It was hard enough to find those two feathers. Where would we get fifty?"

A little while later, Pooh said, "I think I know what the trouble is. You're trying to do Owl things . . . and you should just be Piglet."

"Owl's uncle could make everyone cheer," Piglet said. "Everyone loved him."

"Everyone will love you, too," Pooh said.

"Do you really think so?" Piglet asked.

Pooh smiled. "Yes," he said. "I do."

Piglet practiced hard the next day. Owl got busy, too. He made a long list and read it out loud to Piglet. "First we need an audience. That can be Christopher Robin. Tigger and Roo can open the show. Then we'll have Pooh, then Eeyore, and Rabbit."

"What about me?" Piglet wanted to know.

"You're last," Owl told him. "A good director always saves the best for last. I'm looking forward to the dance of the fifty feathers. Haven't seen it in years."

Piglet said, "Oh d-d-dear!"

That night, Piglet tossed and turned. The next day, he did not want to get out of bed. "I'm sick," he told Pooh, who had stopped by for a visit. "I have the hiccups."

Pooh listened thoughtfully. "Perhaps, Piglet," he said, "you're not sick. Perhaps you're worried about the show."

"I can't dance and I can't sing," Piglet blurted out. "I keep mixing up the words."

"Oh bother," said Pooh. Then he told Piglet, "I may be a bear of very little brain, but I do believe if you do your best, everything will work out—more or less."

For the opening act that afternoon, Tigger and Roo did a bouncy dance. It was exciting, though Kanga had to close her eyes when Roo bounced especially high.

Then Pooh recited a hum about honey.

Next, Eeyore told a long and silly story about his house falling down. The audience laughed and whistled.

"That was wonderfully funny!" Owl patted Eeyore on the back. "Didn't know you had it in you."

"I wasn't trying to be funny," Eeyore said gloomily. "That was supposed to be kind of sad."

At intermission, Kanga served up
the refreshments.

"What talent!" Owl said, happily
munching on a muffin.

Then Rabbit showed off some of his
prize vegetables. He talked about seeds
and dirt and weeding and watering.

And then . . .

. . . Piglet was on. He stood in front of his friends. "This is the dance of the fifty feathers," he said a little shakily, "though Pooh and I only found two." He hopped and danced and waved the feathers around.

One of the feathers tickled Christopher Robin's nose. He sneezed and giggled and sneezed and started to laugh. Soon everyone else was laughing along.

When Piglet's dance was over, the
audience stood up and cheered.

"What a finale!" Owl exclaimed. "My
uncle couldn't have done better."

Pooh said, "You made everyone laugh.
Everyone loved you—but then we always
did."

And Piglet smiled a very big smile.